DON'T BE RUDE!

Philip Blugh

Illustrated by Ayan Mansoori

To my lovely mom, brothers, sister, beautiful wife, and amazing kids.

This Book Belongs To:

_____

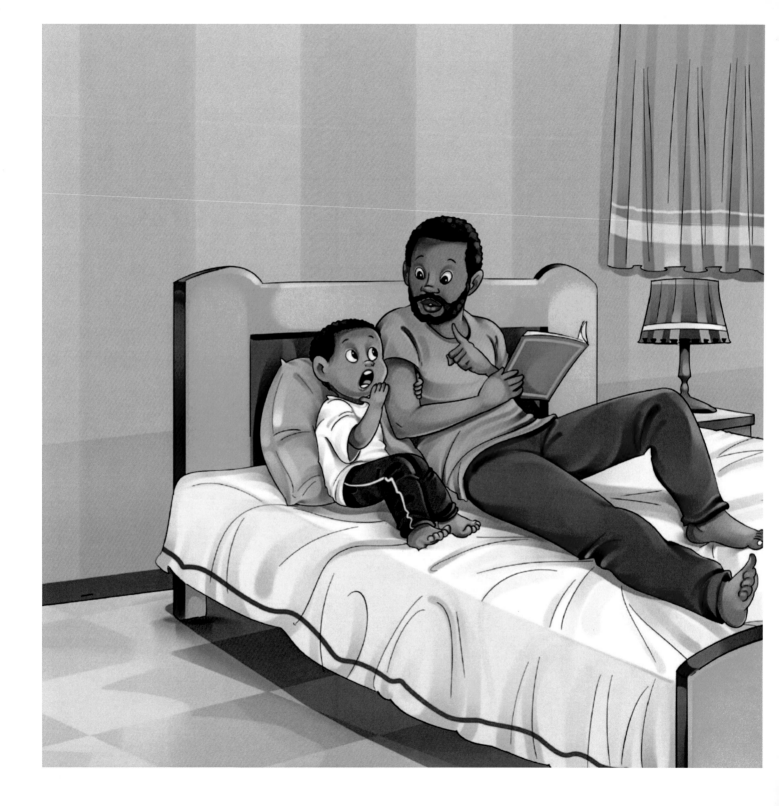

Sometimes I clench my teeth and turn my *head*,
When my Daddy tucks me into *bed*.

He reads me stories to calm me down and sooth my *mood*,
And when he's done, he reminds me that yelling is *rude*.

Sometimes when we go shopping at the *store*,
I ask for this snack, that drink, that candy and *more*.

Daddy tells me to be patient, and that he's not *amused*,
Then, he reminds me that pestering is *rude*.

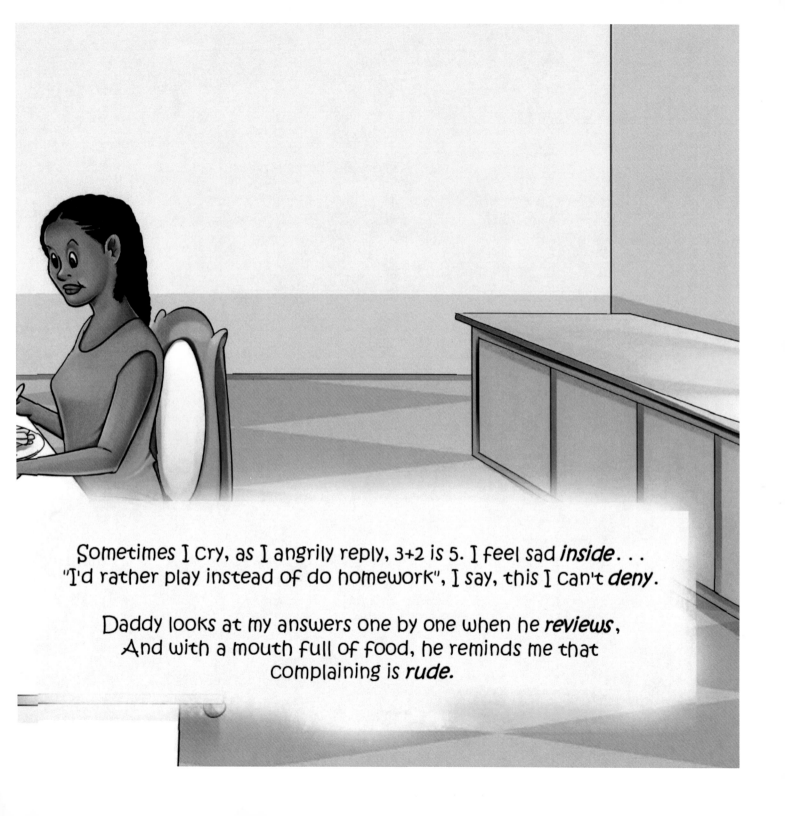

Sometimes I cry, as I angrily reply, 3+2 is 5. I feel sad *inside*. . .
"I'd rather play instead of do homework", I say, this I can't *deny*.

Daddy looks at my answers one by one when he *reviews*,
And with a mouth full of food, he reminds me that
complaining is *rude.*

So. . .

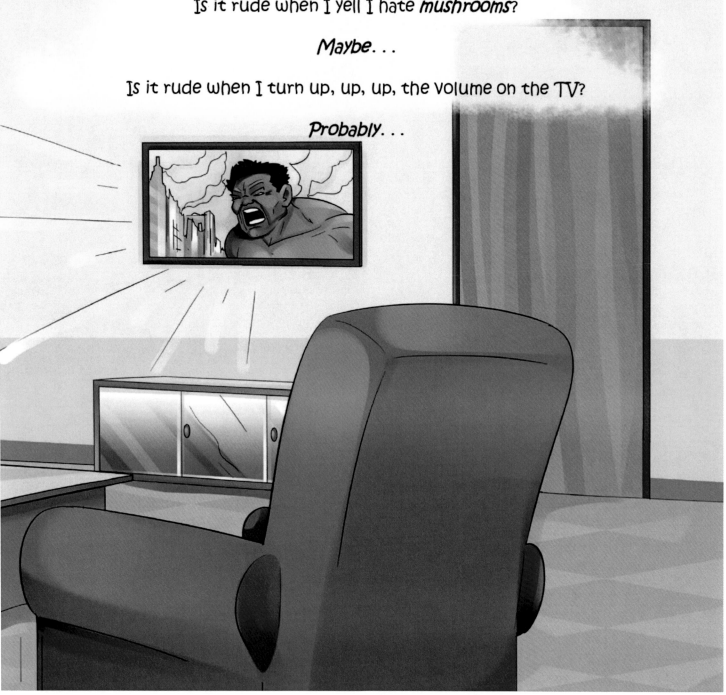

So. . . I stopped thinking to myself and decided to ask my Daddy because I need answers!

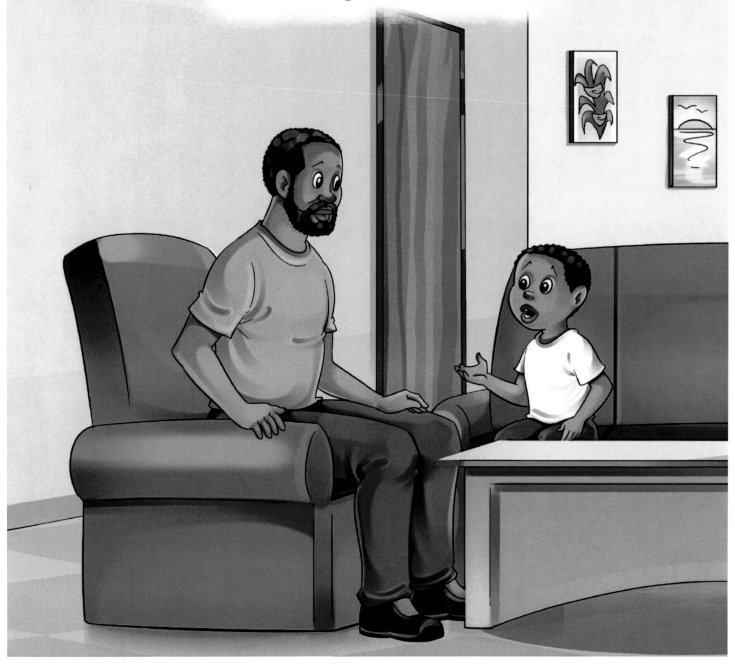

When I asked what it meant to be rude, he looked at me and pointed with his finger to sit down.

He said, "to be rude is to not think about others when you behave the way you do".

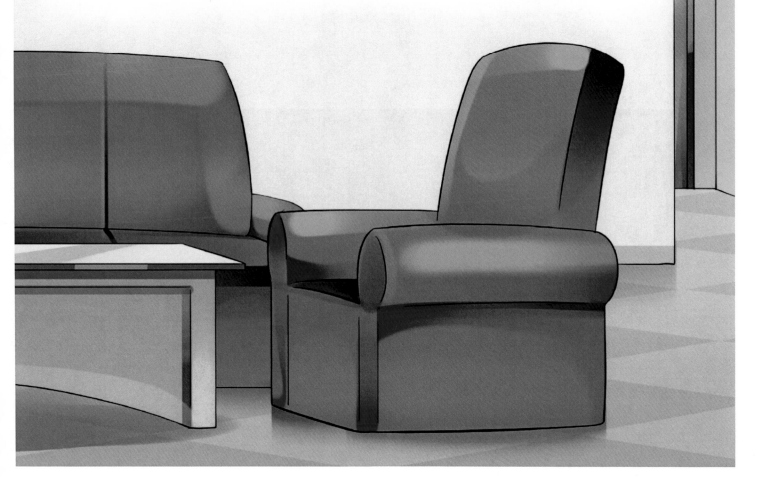

When I'm shopping and you want every snack we walk *past*,
Sometimes I have money only for what's going to *last*.

Foods like mac and cheese, flap jacks, rice, chicken and *peas*,
Not cracker jacks and sour patch candies, that's not what you *need*.

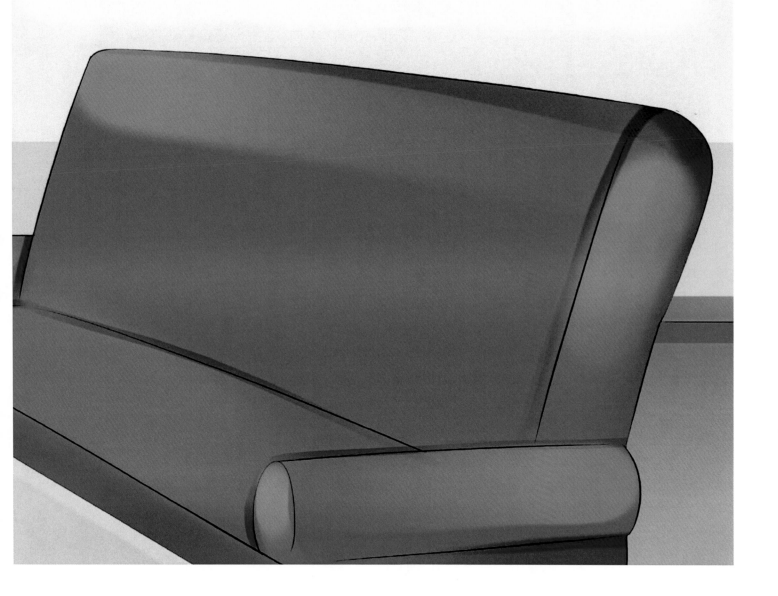

Then he SNEEZED, said "excuse me", and continued. . .

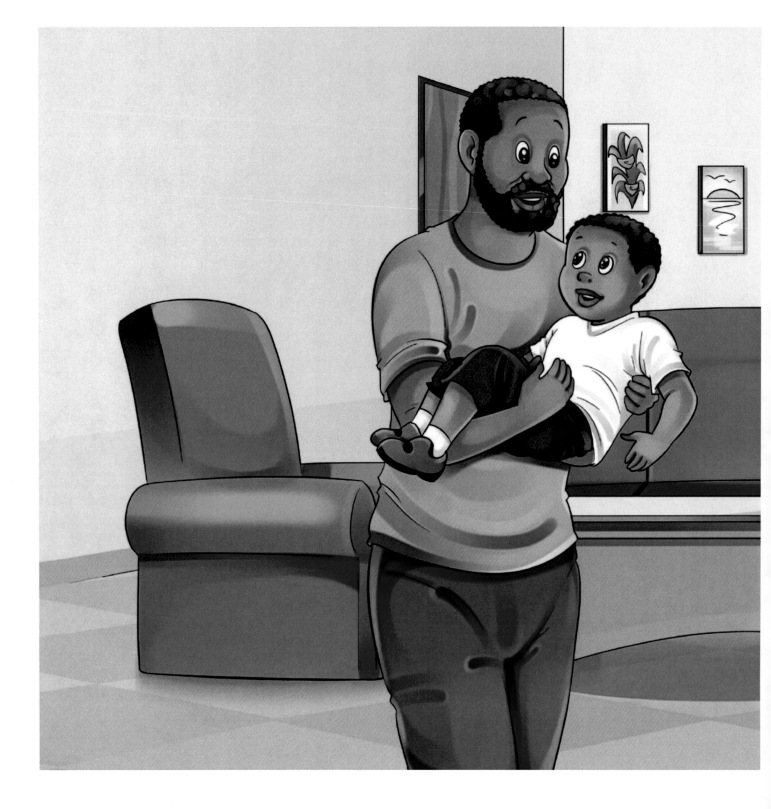

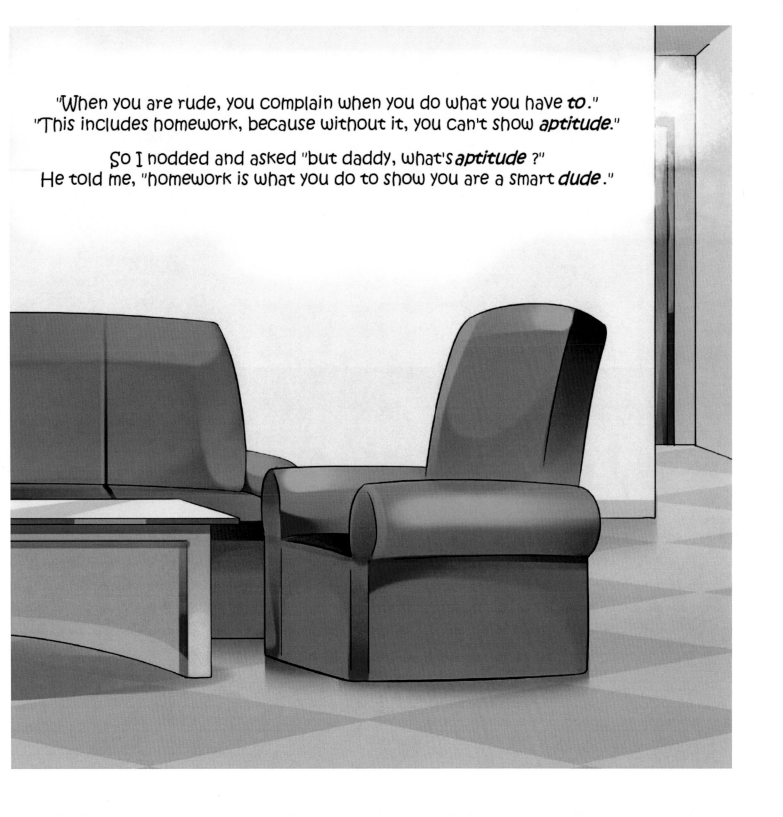

Story Time Lesson

- Have you ever done something rude?

- What can you do if you feel like yelling or being rude?

- Has anyone ever been rude to you? How did it make you feel?

Dear Parents/Reader (A Word from the Author)

Thank you for taking the time to read this book. Please take a moment and leave a review on www.amazon.com. I would love to hear how this book impacted you and your little one.